POINT REYES

MPJ 7/97

POINT REYES

Hello, Amigos!

Hello, Amigos!

By Tricia Brown

Photographs by Fran Ortiz

Henry Holt and Company
New York

Published by Henry Holt and Company, Inc.
521 Fifth Avenue, New York, New York 10175.
Published simultaneously in Canada.

Library of Congress Cataloging in Publication Data
Brown, Tricia.
Hello, amigos!
Summary: Follows a day, a birthday, in the life
of a Mexican American child, who lives with his
family in the Mission district of San Francisco.
1. Mexican Americans—California—San Francisco—
Social life and customs—Juvenile literature.
2. Mexican American children—California—San Francisco
—Juvenile literature.   3. San Francisco (Calif.)—
Social life and customs—Juvenile literature.
[1. Mexican Americans—California—San Francisco—
Social life and customs]   I. Ortiz, Fran, ill.
II. Title.
F869.S39M537   1986   979.4′610046872073   86-9882
ISBN: 0-8050-0090-9

First Edition

Designed by Kate Nichols
Printed in the United States of America
10 9 8 7 6 5 4 3 2 1

ISBN 0-8050-0090-9

Acknowledgments

Muchas gracias to the following persons whose cooperation, support, and
enthusiasm made this book possible: Mr. and Mrs. Roger Valdez and their
children, Gabriel, Claudia, Nancy, Frank, Karen, Leslie, Roger, Jr., and
Raul; the students and faculty of Garfield School, especially Joseph Stal-
lone, principal; Marian Giddings, Spanish bilingual teacher; Anne Kear-
ney; Frank Lempert, program director, Columbia Park Boy's Club;
Charles D. Conley, executive director, Columbia Park Boy's Club; Rever-
end John J. O'Connor, Mission Dolores; Reina A. Parada, La Raza Information Center; Feliz T. Duag, coordinator, Public Information and Public
Affairs Office, San Francisco Unified School District; Nelly Núñez,
Berlitz Translation Services; Peter Connolly, children's librarian, San
Francisco Public Library; Salvador (Chava) Ojeda; Marilyn Welch, Land
of Counterpane; Marvin Martinez; Elyce Kirchener; Jeffrey Rascon;
Steve Essaff; Maria Gonzales; Nydia Maciques-Gomez; Esperanza Bal-
ladares; Catherine Ortiz; Michael Ortiz; Theodore Brown; Barrett Brown;
Andrea Brown; and Marc Cheshire.

To the Roger Valdez family and our other
Mexican-American friends

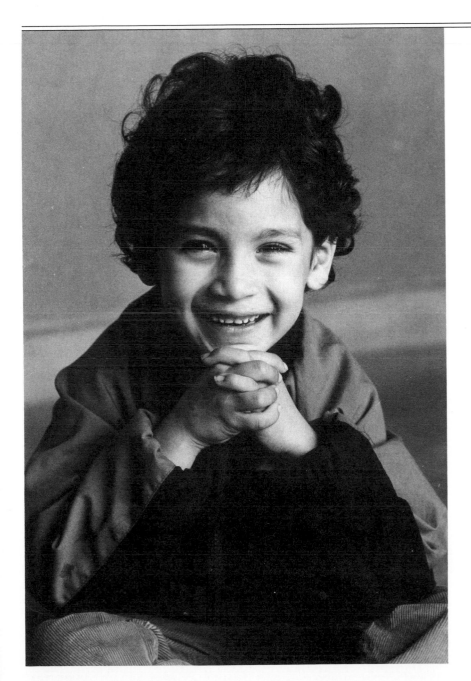

Hello, amigos! My name is Frankie Valdez.

I live in the Mission District in San Francisco with my mother, my father, my three brothers, and my four sisters.

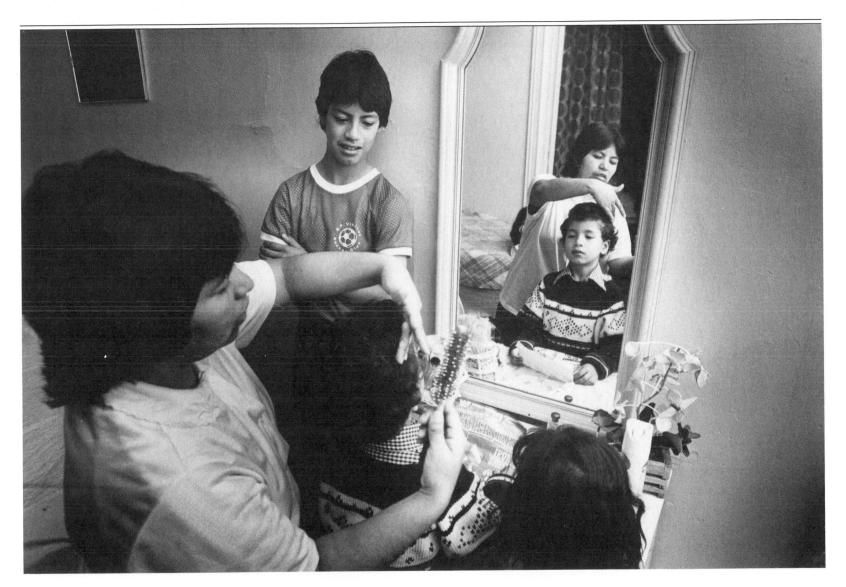

Today is my birthday. As my mother helps me get ready for school, my brother Gabriel wishes me a Feliz Cumpleaños—that means "Happy Birthday" in Spanish.

I feel so happy today. When I get home from school we will have my birthday party.

My sister Nancy and I go to the same school. The bus ride takes a long time.

I like to look out the window as we drive through the city.

I always sit with my best friend, Marvin Martinez.

Marvin hurt his arm. At school I help him fix his sling. Maybe I'll be a doctor when I grow up.

There's the school bell. It's time for breakfast. Mmmmmmm . . . this leche is good.

At my school the first and second graders are in the same classroom. Some of us speak Spanish at home, and we learn English here at school.

Our first lesson is math. Sometimes I don't get it.

Mrs. Giddings, my teacher, helps me to understand. She speaks
Spanish, too.

Next we have recess. I love to play outside!

After recess we study English. I like English best when I get the right answer.

During science Mrs. Giddings shows a movie about mammals. My sister likes it, but it makes me sleepy.

During P.E. we play kickball. Because it's my birthday, Mrs. Giddings lets me serve first.

After P.E. everyone surprises me with a birthday cake and a corona to wear.

I like to eat lunch with my friends, but today I eat quickly and clean up early.

At my school we go home after lunch.

I can't wait to get home and have my birthday fiesta.

Yippee! I'm finally home.

My mom says it will be a few hours before the party starts. She wants to make some guacamole and sends me to the market for some avocados.

When I get back I want to go to the Columbia Park Boy's Club. My mom says that before I go, I need to finish my homework. Luckily, my older brother, Gabriel, and my older sister, Claudia, help me.

Then Gabriel and I walk to the Boy's Club.

Frank, the program director, is teaching me how to play pool.

After my lesson I try to wait for Gabriel and his friend, Tyrone, to finish their game of foosball.

When we get home it's almost time for my party! I change into my party clothes and put on the corona my teacher made for me. I watch my mother mash the avocados with her molcajate.

Hmmm . . . delicioso!

My mother and father invite our family, friends, and neighbors to eat our favorite Mexican food—enchiladas, frijoles refritos, arroz, tortillas, and, of course, the delicious guacamole.

Chava, my father's friend, stops by to sing some songs on his way to work. He is a mariachi and sings in a nearby restaurant.

My favorite food is my birthday cake!

After we eat I get to break the piñata.

When the piñata breaks, everyone gets to pick up the candy.

It has been a wonderful day. Papa and I walk to our church. He helps me light a candle, and I count my blessings.

Glossary

amigos (ah-**mee**-goes): friends

arroz (ah-**rohs**): rice

corona (kor-**oh**-nah): crown

delicioso (deh-lee-**syo**-so): delicious

enchiladas (en-chee-**lah**-das): Mexican dish made with tortillas, meat, chili sauce, and cheese

Feliz Cumpleaños (Feh-**lees** Kum-play-**an**-yos): Happy Birthday

fiesta (**fyes**-tah): feast, party, holiday

frijoles refritos (free-**hoe**-lehs reh-**free**-tohs): refried beans

guacamole (gwa-kah-**mo**-lay): Mexican salad or sauce made with avocados, lemon juice, onions, herbs, and chili peppers

leche (**leh**-chay): milk

mariachi (mah-ree-**ah**-chee): a member of a strolling band of musicians in Mexico

molcajate (mol-kah-**hah**-teh): stone gourd used by Mexican women for grinding food

muchas gracias (**moo**-chahs **grah**-syas): many thanks; thank you very much

piñata (peen-**yah**-tah): papier-mâché, candy-filled toy that hangs from the ceiling and is broken with a long stick

tortillas (tor-**tee**-yas): Mexican flat bread made of flour or corn

About the Author

Tricia Brown's first book, *Someone Special, Just Like You*, published by Holt, Rinehart and Winston in May 1984, was listed as one of the notable 1984 Children's Trade Books in the field of social studies and won the 1985 Book Award from the President's Committee on Employment of the Handicapped. *Hello, Amigos!* is her second book. She has traveled extensively throughout Latin America and speaks Spanish fluently. Currently she is working on her third book and is a substitute teacher. She lives in San Francisco on Telegraph Hill with her husband, an architect, and their six-year-old son.

About the Photographer

Fran Ortiz, an award-winning photojournalist, was also the photographer for *Someone Special, Just Like You*. He is currently the Director of Photography for *The San Francisco Examiner*. Throughout his twenty-year career he has photographed for many magazines, among them *Time*, *Life*, *Harper's Bazaar*, and *National Geographic*. In 1981 he was nominated for the Pulitzer Prize for his social documentary on the Mono Indians. He lives in Kensington, California, with his wife and two-year-old son.